Unwavered Faith

By:

TIFFINI JOHNSON

UNWAVERED FAITH

Cover Design, Editing and Formatting by:
Ya Ya Ya Creative – ww.yayayacreative.com

ISBN No. 978-0-578-21580-8

PRINTED AND BOUND IN THE UNITED STATES OF AMERICA

Table of Contents

Introduction

Waking up every day was killing me! I wanted to scream out for help, but in my mind, the people around me could not help. I was becoming physically, emotionally and mentally unstable. I made the decision to write down my thoughts, to get them out of my head, and the result is this book. As you read, you will take a journey through my thoughts and emotions on my road to personal success. This book is for anyone out there who needs help praying through the pain, the struggle, the doubt and the depression.

This book is broken down into three different sections. Trials and Tribulations, Pray Without Ceasing, and Commanding My Life. I am just expressing my gratitude towards prayer and how God has brought me this far. I could have given up a long time ago. I know my pain and struggles are not any better or worse than anyone else's, this is just what I have lived. I want to inspire and help others who are dealing with a life of struggle, pain, disappointments, lack, and setbacks. I cannot even begin to give you an explanation of "Why" people go through what they go through. I am tearing up as I write this because I know how hard and exhausting it is to find a way to keep going when you feel like you have nothing left. The statement "What doesn't kill you, makes you stronger," is beyond true. I know for a fact that there is a reason for adversity. While there are challenges I would have loved to skip, I just know that we go through certain situations for a reason. We are being qualified for abundance and increase, and we need to be prepared with the right mindset and strategies to be as successful as possible. So join me on a journey through my experiences and I hope that you will understand why it is so important to Pray Through your current circumstances, then keep praying once it gets better. Command Your Life and learn from your failures and trials and live the life you have always wanted. Not every day will be filled with sunshine and rainbows, but you are strong enough get through it to.

Facebook Fan Page
Unwavered Faith

Please leave your reviews on my Fan Page and Amazon.com. I hope I inspire you to keep going and never give up, because the struggles do not last forever. Remember, faith without work is dead.

https://www.facebook.com/unwaveredfaith/

Trials & Tribulations

It is Always a Good Time to Pray

I prolonged writing this book because I wanted to end with "NOW I AM A SUCCESFUL MULTI-MILLIONARE, BLAH, BLAH BLAH" and list all of my accomplishments, but that is not the way God works. If I had continued to wait for the good times, or my idea of success, I would have missed the blessings that this book has brought to me, and will bring to anyone else having a hard time praying through. Praying through is a mental, physical, and emotional daily battle. You might be living up life some days and in a state of deep depression the next. Anything can give you the momentum to keep going and at the same time you can be brought right back down again. I just want you to start working on your faith. By no means will it happen overnight, or even a year from now. You have to have a definite desire to build your faith, which will then help you to reach your **"Next Right Move"**, as the amazing Oprah Winfrey would say. Deciding to work on daily self-improvement was the biggest gift I could have ever given myself.

I took a training class at Keller Williams, instructed by Karen Sacco, that walked participants through the

Miracle Morning Life SAVERS. It was the best investment of time I have ever made. *The Miracle Morning* by Hal Elrod was a slap in the face to how much I limit myself. I realized it was all my fought that I was not living up to my full potential. I needed that slap (and yes that last sentence was hard to say, write, re-read, and realize for myself) and even more so, I needed to remove all limiting beliefs. Growing up I was always organized, even to the point of being OCD (obsessive compulsive disorder), but I never looked at this disorder as a hindrance. I am fearfully and wonderfully made and appreciate God for it. While reading *The Miracle Morning* I was simultaneously reading Mark Batterson's *The Circle Maker*. *The Circle Maker* was helping me to learn how to pray **bold** prayers. I will read and reread both of these books for the rest of my life because the impact that these books have had on me is life changing. Praying without ceasing and being determined to live and not just exist has become my sole focus. In praying for change in my life, I realized that my mental state was in complete dysfunction. I had thoughts of suicide, bitterness, and low self-esteem. I did not want to invest time in any personal relationship because I had nothing going on for my life financially. I felt like the ultimate bum. So I began praying for mental strength.

My Mental State

Mentally, I am back and forth between being positive and going insane. I feel uplifted and then the littlest thing reminds me of my current circumstances and how much I have to overcome. I think of the impending battles and I get scared. I look at other people in much worse positions than I am in and I do not want to feel ungrateful, but I am truly exhausted. I feel like I am taking risks and going for my dreams and I have nothing to show for it. I work daily on self-improvement in an effort to gain more confidence, acknowledge my many accomplishments and how far I have come, and to be at peace with where I am in my life while consciously striving for better. I know struggling is not the story of my life and I know that mentally I am my own worst enemy. I pray every day for my peace and structure. I can and will do better, while enjoying my life. I watch reality shows where people chase their dreams with great financial barriers. People encourage them saying "The money is coming" and "Keep doing what you're doing, you'll make it." Pause. That is so hard when you are living paycheck to paycheck, no car, my lease will be up soon and I have no money to move and don't make enough money to save. I feel like that line in that City High song "Everyday I wake up hopin' to die," and I know that is deep but the unknown is so scary. There is no one that can help me make it another day, no one except God and myself.

Mentally, I am a work in progress. My biggest fear is being homeless and having to go back to Cincinnati. I finally live in a city where I want to be and cannot imagine having to start over. Going home to Cincinnati would be easy. I would have a support system to get established, yet I struggle with the thought of going home. I just really do not want to ask God for the strength to get through something else. This might sound depressing and forgive me; I am just letting you know that even through my dysfunction, I still pray, and I find joy in the little things. Daily and even hourly prayer gives me hope.

Pride

In all honesty, pride is the reason I did not want to go back to Cincinnati. In Florida, most of the people that I have welcomed into my life are striving for something better. They have goals and they welcome change. In Cincinnati, I often found myself encountering people from my past, friends and family, which did not have goals or ambition. Just the thought of being around certain people was draining. Then I realized pride was the reason I did not want anything to do with going back home. Yes, it would be easier. I would have a way to get around and save money, but the thought of encountering people from my past that have not evolved their way of thinking was gut-wrenching.

A trip home, during which I saw how much the city itself had changed gave me a revitalized sense of hope. I prayed for a new strategy to expand my real estate investing career in Cincinnati instead of Florida for the time being. I changed my perception and evolved my way of thinking to see moving home as a bigger advantage then just living at home and saving money. I prayed to remove this high level of pride from my life daily. I needed to change myself, God made sure that I was going to move when He told me to move. I learned that I could not just do my own thing and trust God only when He is working in the direction I wanted Him to go.

God making me move back to Cincinnati was a reality check. I am thankful that God is not through with me yet and that He is making sure I am prepared for the magnified blessings coming my way. It is not always easy to trust God and I often get caught up doing what I think is right rather than truly listening and following God's promptings. I did not even realize that pride was the reason I was hurting myself. God had intended to put me in position earlier, I just had to wake up and follow His direction. Forgive me, Lord, and may You please continue to work on me. This book was written in the order of which I felt God was speaking to me at that time. As you continue to read and I hope you are inspired to pray for a renewed mind and a new strategy toward your victory.

God is Not Real

God is not real. That may seem pretty harsh for a book that is teaching you about praying through, but as I said I am taking you on a journey, my journey. I wasn't always saved. A long time ago, when my sisters and I were younger, we lived in a really nice home in Cincinnati, Ohio. We were going through a rough week and my older sister felt compelled to write God is Not Real on the ceiling of our shared bedroom. Looking back, that was a truly great assumption. My sisters and I had been through so much before the age of ten. In the back of my mind, I never wanted to make it worse, but trust me it got worse and then it out did itself. I was looking up at the ceiling thinking, "yeah, that's about right."

Prayer on the other hand has been a part of my life since I was a child. The two things I always knew how to do, be persuasive and pray. I would feel bad if I ever missed a nightly prayer. Eventually I realized that I could pray anytime, not just at night. I was very optimistic when I was younger, always hoping that things would work out for the best. I do feel that my sisters and I had to grow up too fast, and time and time again we did what we had to do and not what we wanted to do but I really just wanted to be a child and enjoy life. I didn't want to lose hope and accept that my life would always be this rough. I knew that there had to be a God and we were children, so it was very hard for me to realize that we had to be our own rescuers. Being so young, we really didn't know how to rescue ourselves but I prayed that one day it would get better, one day it would no longer be a fight or a battle. I have learned that when God is qualifying, you there is no day off from ups and downs. Without bad days, we cannot know what a really great day feels like.

My goal was to not have to live in my childhood home in Cincinnati again, and thankfully, God has always provided a place for me to live, whether in Cincy or elsewhere. I am hopeful, and will do everything that I can, to not give up. I just have to hang on a little longer. My breakthrough is coming and I have to stay faithful no matter what. Finally, I have to remember that God doesn't have to prove Himself to us, we have to prove ourselves to Him. God is already worthy of our praise.

Negative Outcomes

I have experienced so many unfortunate things in my life that I have truly lost count. Whenever I am with my sisters and we reminisce over all we have been through, I am thankful for the things that no longer linger in my mind. I am in constant spiritual warfare. I mentally battle for my soul every day, even now. I know that I will battle this until it is my time for life everlasting.

When you lose count of your troubles that is one thing, but when you are having a good day and are convinced that disappointment must be on its way, then that is a whole different issue. I love to visualize greatness happening to me and I constantly dream of a better life. In that same moment, I dream of something bad, frustrating or catastrophic happening to me during that time as well. The life that I have lived thus far causes me to automatically assume that something bad is going to happen, in some form or another. As sad as that is, I have realized my tendency to do this and I am currently reprogramming myself to think differently. Fortunately, God helped me realize that I was plugging in my own heartaches. I can't think of any stretch of time where I didn't have some form of a bad situation coming or going. That leads me to my prayer of believing that great things will happen to me constantly. Not sometimes, not once in a while, but constantly. I pray for a great life, a life filled with abundance and increase, a life of expectancy and devotion to God for keeping it great. I now set different reminders on my phone or iPad® telling me that it is my set time, my due season, season of favor, etc. I am slowly but surely programming myself to change my way of thinking and living throughout the day with little reminders to keep me at peace and focused. Staying at rest is easier said than done, but battle for your peace, work on your goals and ***never give up***.

I Need Help

I am thankful for my one of my best friends, Nathan. I needed help financially and literally felt like dying when I needed to ask for help. There is nothing worse than bring indebted to someone, especially a friend. I am incredibly thankful for his help, financially and mentally, in my time of need. I was happy to have someone to talk me off the ledge of life when I needed them the most. I felt like I was going crazy. I would study the businesses that I wanted to pursue, I would research and get all my ducks in a row and never get anywhere. I was organized, I kept a clean home, I prayed, I helped other people and I couldn't catch a break to save my life.

To this day, I cannot imagine going through life being mediocre and just surviving. I have always wanted to live and travel, to spend time with my family and friends. While on my journey, I have missed out on so much involving the lives of my family and friends. There were so many times when I wanted to go to a family function, or when I wanted to help my family financially during a rough time, but I needed help myself first. I know that life has a way of working itself out and blessings come in all forms. All I can ask is that on those rough days, turn on some gospel music, say a prayer by yourself, write down your thoughts to get them out of your head, and begin your process of change. Re-program your mind to focus on prosperity, increase, self-improvement, and humility. Remember how far you have come while making a conscious effort to do better daily. Ask for help when you can and always search for a way to reach your goals, no matter your circumstances. Make a plan, give your self-definite dates to save, achieve certain goals, leave a job, start a business, search for funding, etc. You must have a plan for success. Nothing is unattainable; you just have to go out of your way to make it happen.

 Tiffini Johnson—Unwavered Faith

Pray Without Ceasing

Patience

When things do not go the way you wanted them to, that is God intending to inspire you. God is allowing you to dream bigger, to move in a different direction, to evolve your thoughts. When you move on the promises God has put in your heart, no matter what age, then you begin to open up supernatural blessings that are magnified as you continue to pursue your passion.

Most people do not have patience and it is amazing to me that many people go out of their way to not work on the issues in their life. Meditating and being accustomed to change has helped me to grow my patience daily with what the day may bring. As far as patience for reaching my level of success—"God is not through with me yet," said in my best Steve Harvey voice. Setting goals and striving to achieve them is what motivates me to wake up and win. I love Mondays and beginning a new week on my spiritual, emotional, mental, financial and relationship quest gives me life. I am excited for my future and being an inspiration to others.

I have so many dreams and goals that I want to see come to pass, for society, the government, how our judicial system is run, an increased minimum wage, and so on. My dreams are not just personal they are global.

My dreams carry so much weight that I know the only person that can make them happen is God. I have dreams where I am looking so far into the future that I want my grandchildren to reap the benefits. Have patience, work on your goals, surround yourself with people doing better than you and fail forward. Learn what works and what doesn't, then revise your plan. Failure is not an ending, it is the beginning of a new way of reaching your goal.

Obedience

I was trying to avoid this passage, but God is telling me to be honest and I could not claim to be finished with this book without it. I am the "obedient when it is convenient" person. I will find an excuse to do something that I want to do in a heartbeat. I am starting a segment of prayer today, right now, because I know that I make excuses and I need to be forever moving forward in all aspects of my life, not just some. Be brutally honest with God when you stop to say your prayer to be more obedient, and as the weeks progress, take action to live soberly and righteously in this present world. There are so many worldly lust moments where you can say "Today I won't participate in that activity."

I personally really enjoy going to strip clubs. I go to strip clubs and turn up like I'm at LIV on Sundays in Miami. I make the excuses that I want their wings or to see a certain celebrity or just go and chill. Strip clubs are a worldly lust. I am happy that I made steps to change that part of my life, but I am a work in progress for so many worldly lusts. I am sitting here thinking about how much I use profanity and how I am so quick to tell someone to "Shut the f### up and get your life together." The pot calling the kettle black! I have always liked to use profanity and my mom is a professional when it is time to cuss someone out, her children included. I learned from the best. Shout out to my mom on that note, but it is my choice to use profanity and my choice to begin to use it less, amongst other things. Wow. I cannot believe how many things I make excuses for just so I can express myself in the way I want to. I am not saying that I will never use profanity again, I am just going to make a daily conscious effort to not use profanity as much as I have been. For now, I will incorporate a prayer of obedience to keep in tune with my star player and my quest to everlasting life. No more excuses, no more selfishness, and truly commanding my day for greatness.

Hungry

I was not hungry. Not in the sense of being eager to be successful, or put out my new project and ambitions. I mean literally *I was hungry*. There is nothing like being invited to hang out with your friends but you can't go because you have no money and the only thing you have eaten since yesterday was a pack of chicken flavored ramen noodles. I would have to tell people that I could not go if the place involved food because I had not eaten an adequate meal in days. Hunger pains are the worst.

There have been several times in my life when I have been too broke to eat more than one meal a day, but for now I'll focus on the past year. I really had hope that once I had my real estate license, actively marketed my business, learned to set goals, and created my database, that God would come through for me. I had been struggling for so long that I figured it had to be time for some good breaks. I would get leads, follow up, care about helping people and time and time again people would not be ready to move forward. My phone bill was due, rent was due, I needed food, and I still had hope. I took a risk, I walked by faith and not by sight, I was determined, yet *nothing*. Then I took out payday loans, borrowed money, created a *GoFundMe* drive to raise money, applied to grants, found capital to begin flipping houses, and every time I thought I had finally caught a break, it wasn't enough. When I found the capital, I needed my LLC which was another hundred plus dollars to obtain, then I needed a DBA, then no one donated to my fund, and so on. I did so much research, created presentations, delivered my ideas, and just never caught a break. I got so tired of eating ramen noodles that at one point, I just stopped eating. I was only eating one time a day so to stop eating wasn't a huge leap. I didn't have a car so I was either walking, riding my bike, or catching the bus, in the Florida heat, with no food in my stomach. I felt like I was dying, but I was still optimistic that God would not let me starve to death so I applied for a job and eventually got hired at the Marriott. I felt like such a failure because I knew it was going to be harder to really focus on my real estate dreams with another full time job that barely paid enough to cover my monthly rent.

I just knew that if I walked by faith and followed my dreams, God would make a way out of no way for me to succeed and finally be able to live, not just exists. I went back to working, still promoting, no longer hungry, but on a severely low budget and I lost hope. I was still praying everyday and with what little hope existed, I tried to remain optimistic. I use to lay down on the floor and shake and cry because I felt like I was going crazy. I was so angry and embarrassed and depressed. I just wanted to die. I have no children and with this new job, I made sure I had life insurance (I couldn't afford anything else) so I was good to die. I thought about suicide a million times. I was having a nervous breakdown everyday. There is nothing worse than talking yourself into going to work at a place that doesn't stimulate your soul in the least, but through it all, I kept praying. I talked to God every day. I wished I had someone else to talk to and that is why I decided to write this book. I needed to talk about my issues, get them out my head, and let them go. This book is the "letting it go" chapter in my life. I know that there is a reason I have to go through this, and Lord knows I would rather just die, but I am so hopeful, inspired everyday by the littlest things that I truly feel that God is telling me to hold on a little longer and watch what He is about to do for me.

I am crying my eyes out writing this, but I have made it through worse, believe it or not. I just do not want to be bitter and I hope I do not seem ungrateful. I appreciate having a roof over my head and my bike and everything that I have. I just don't want to be this talented, positive and inspiring, a go-getter, and still be struggling. Seriously, ever since I read *The Miracle Morning* by Hal Elrod and started pursuing all of my dreams while removing all limiting beliefs; you can't tell me nothing. Even if I am dead broke, anything extra I have is going to my dreams. You only get one life and if I die tomorrow, I can say with conviction that I am pursuing everything that I wanted. I graduated from North Carolina Central University with a Bachelors in Business, I am a Realtor, I am a Self-Published Author of not one, but *two books*, I am an aspiring full time entrepreneur and I have inspired more people in one day than most people do in a lifetime. So when I look back and reflect, I am not doing too bad. So I thank you God for perseverance because that was just this year. I have had a whole lifetime of obstacles that I have overcome and *I AM POWERFUL BEYOND MEASURE!!!*

Suicide

This is where it gets a little deep, but I am still living by the grace of God and I pray every day to be able to reach a point in my life where I am fully living in prosperity and abundance. I told you previously that with the challenges in my life, I had thought about suicide a million times. I know people reading this might say "Going through challenges is temporary and that is no reason to consider suicide," and you are entitled to your opinion. In my mind, it feels like I have been struggling for 27 years. I have taken risks and believed in something better, I have done what most people could not with the lack of resources at my disposal and I am still broke and struggling. "The struggle is real," is an understatement.

I thought about all kinds of ways of killing myself. I just did not want to feel pain. I wanted it to be instant. I told my younger sister over Facebook Messenger that if I died, I want a graveside service. Everyone needed to wear white or green (my favorite colors) and I wanted "Heaven" by Jaimie Foxx to be playing in the background. I didn't want anyone to be sad but I knew that I would be creating another sad moment in my family's life and that it was selfish. My family would have to ship my body back to Cincinnati, which could cause additional grief. I would never actually have killed myself, but I did think about it often. Thank God for my friends that brought me back to reality when I felt like I want to jump. I am so grateful for laughter and I pray for peace, patience and mental strength daily. I pray that those thoughts would leave my mind for good and that my life would get better. I was so exhausted and some days were worse than others, but I have made it through. God doesn't call the qualified; He qualifies the called!

If you have thoughts of suicide please get help immediately. National Suicide Prevention Lifeline is available 24/7, 1-800-273-8255 or http://suicidepreventionlifeline.org.

What Am I Not Doing Right

Every time something went wrong or I didn't receive thousands of sales or if something I was praying for didn't happen the way I wanted, I would ask myself *"What am I not doing right?"* Am I not praying hard enough? Am I not faithful enough? Did I say the wrong prayer? What am I doing wrong? You name it, I thought it. God works on His own time. God does or doesn't do things in order to push you in the right direction, to inspire you, and to make you be the change in your circumstances. You have to be the change that your life needs. You cannot rely on other people to make your life better. If you don't make a conscious daily effort to change your mindset, remove all limits, and improve yourself as a whole, then what do you wake up for? I never understood why people say I'm not a morning person or I don't like Mondays because it's all a choice at how you perceive something. You can choose to enjoy the life you have while making a conscious effort to change your circumstance, or go day by day just enduring what life has to offer. I personally love surrounding myself with ambitious people with huge goals. I am one of the most ambitious people I know because I never settle. I have so many challenges in my life and I will go out of my way to learn something on my own and put forth an effort to achieve a task big or small. I make sure that if I don't know something, I exhaust all options before I give up or ask someone for help. I know this has contributed to my success. I am compelled to learn. I read multiple books daily and constantly build my skills. I use to think that I wasn't talented, or that my only talent was my organization skills. Everything has to have a place and a purpose or it has to go. I de-clutter my life often to make room for bigger and better goals, dreams, and desires. It is extremely rare that I do not achieve a goal. When I have a challenge, I take a step back, breathe, listen to music, or take a day off and strategize. I remind myself that things don't happen overnight and I have to make sacrifices and live without some things to make my dreams a reality.

What am I not doing right? Looking back on those moments when I would ask this question—those were the times God was telling me to build my faith and trust Him and His timing. When I really think about all God has done for me; He really was on time when I truly needed Him. I am grateful and I work every day to build my faith and trust in God. I have my moments when I feel I have nothing left and every time, I freak out or beat myself up mentally, but God never lets me quit. I love working for myself, being creative and answering to me and only me. Of course, I have coaches and people who hold me accountable for my actions to make me better, but I love the idea that I have no limits. There is no limit to my creativity, income, relationships, goals, self-improvement, nothing. Entrepreneurs love Mondays and typically get up early, ready to take over the world every day. I cannot even explain how freeing it is to love what I do and get paid for it. Strive for greatness every day. Enjoy life. Do not just endure it. You only get one life and so many people live un-happily because they are scared to get out of their comfort zone. I personally could never understand that. People will stay in relationships that are dead, jobs that they hate, live in mediocrity, yet get defensive when someone asks about their life. I just don't understand. We each get one life; we cannot do this over. Be the change that your life needs. It is not going to be easy, but that is why you have to improve yourself daily! Make an *EFFORT!* What are you waiting for? You are never too old, too young, too handicapped, too whatever. Your excuses are to start changing your life. Remove the limits in your life and do something every day to better yourself and your circumstances. Get a financial education, read daily, meditate, write, pray, study, do whatever it takes to build your skills. Not everyone has talent; BUT EVERYONE CAN BUILD THEIR SKILLS. God has been making a way out of no way for centuries and God works in mysterious ways. He can bring you out better than you were before. Just keep praying through. It is going to be better than alright.

Other People's Limits

This is my favorite part. Other people are going to try to limit you left and right. Always bet on yourself. Never let anyone tell you what you cannot do or how you should be doing things they know nothing about. While reading the powerful *Think and Grow Rich* by Napoleon Hill, I discovered that I have a burning desire and a definite mindset for success. I also realized that I have multiple passions and wanted to experience success (aka, get paid greatly) for what I love to do in all of those outlets. I had people tell me because I hadn't sold a house in the first year of earning my real estate license that I should do something different. The negativity and suggestion of being someone's employee for the rest of my life started to roll in, but I knew that I had a passion for real estate and passive income streams and abundance. I had to align my faith with my definite desire to succeed in real estate. So I became focused. Now mind you, I didn't have a car, I made just enough to pay my rent, eat, and pay one or two bills. I put a few clothes on layaway from time to time, but I wasn't going to let those challenges be an excuse to say I couldn't be successful in real estate. I could not pay my board dues, phone bill, etc. but if I let those challenges be my excuse to quit, then I never really wanted to succeed in real estate.

When I told people I was writing my first book, *Fantasy, Short Stories to Excite* I was excited and just knew everyone would want to buy my book. I put so much effort and cleverness into my stories that I knew just writing it would make people want to read it. Also the eBook was only $4.99. Who doesn't have five dollars? I was broke and I could buy that! With that said, I did not have a record number of sales my first week, yet I remained encouraged. I advertised where I could, converted my real estate database to mail chimp so I could advertise all of my businesses with the same subscriber lists, I learned to not quit when you reach your dream and the finances are not reflecting it. I watched Joel Osteen on YouTube and he had a broadcast where he said that could be God inspiring you to go further or pursue another dream, it is not a settling point. Continue growing. Everything takes time and you have to do whatever you can to stay encouraged. I began to pray even more. I felt resentful and angry and my emotional state was failing. Once again I questioned what was I not doing right. I was literally by myself all the time, which means I was in my head being my own worst enemy. I can say "Don't do that, find another outlet," but I would be wasting ink. Work on your faith, battle for your mental and emotional state of mind. I had my best friend, Nathan, to talk to on my worst days because business wise we related the most. We both were striving for something better despite of our circumstances and he helped me off the ledge a few times, on my worst days. In my mind I would rather die than give up and remain mediocre, struggling, and barely making it. I listen to gospel music on Pandora. The Kirk Franklin station has encouraged me more days then I can count. I also had my ratchet music, R&B or any Wale's album or mixtape. Music brought me back to life and allowed me to dream and escape reality. Music pulled me from destruction of myself and I am thankful for the healing, the inspiration, and just the good vibes that music brings to the soul. I love music that you can feel which is why I am a big fan of R&B, Gospel, Wale, and anything that I can relate to and evolve with. So please don't beat yourself up if you achieve a goal and the money doesn't flow in right away. Pray, stay in faith, find an outlet, read, listen to music, and talk to someone if you can. Then breathe.

Settling

Deep breath. I am going to speak about why I refuse to settle. While writing this book and looking at my life, I have faced several challenges. Most people wouldn't go to work if they didn't have a car, but I would get on my bike every day at 3:45 a.m. and get to work on time. I could not afford to pay my phone bill often so most of my communication was through email. My friends have to message me on Facebook or Skype just to talk with me, but I make it work every day. I was able to email my editor everything I needed her to do for my first and second book. I was able to self-publish my book without physically speaking to her once. I promote my businesses every day and email or message people who have any questions about products. I have truly learned to live with the bare minimum. Knowing my circumstances, I avoid having to talk to too many people, because I'm embarrassed that my phone is off. People look at you like "How are you surviving?" I do not quit and I know I take a lot of risks, but I really want to enjoy going to work and not having to talk myself into walking through the door every day. I appreciate being accustomed to change because it is very little things that I freak out over. If I can't do something because I don't have the money then I am not spending my last or faking like I got it. I just won't be there.

Knowing all the obstacles in my life I would constantly settle. I would never do anything for me in the terms of fun because everything went to making my dreams come true. I constantly invested in books, or advertising, or time going to financial seminars, and I just found myself so focused on making it that I lost just being me at times. I never went anywhere, I felt like there was no point to finding someone to date because I wasn't proud of myself financially. I didn't want to need a man for anything. Just the thought of asking a guy I'm dating for help or money would have mentally broke me. That would have been the last straw and I would have physically given up. Prayer truly keeps me from going too far. Dreaming of a better life and visualizing my success inspires me to stay motivated. My daily self-improvement exercises allow me to enjoy, rather than just endure the process. I know it is hard and at times you feel like you have nothing left. So think about this; if you had nothing left, you would be dead already.

Your Circumstances

Your battle is not someone else's battle, and most people do not understand how to react to your situation. I use to go door knocking to promote my business. Depending on the day, I would have to get on my bike, ride it to the bus stop, get on two or three different buses, and then walk a section of a neighborhood, door knocking a hundred homes. Then I would get back on the bus to go home, all in the Florida heat. I am not complaining, but if I couldn't make it one day, then damn, I couldn't make it. I would push myself and think I could do it all, but it just wasn't possible. Then I would feel bad and beat myself up. Eventually I realized I can't do everything for everyone. Usually, I am the first person to reach out to help someone and I try my best to stick with them until they get it, but most people have more than me. Don't get discouraged. Realize that some days, you have to do what is best for you. Seriously, battle for your peace of mind, have patience, remember that not everyone knows how to deal with your situation because they are not living it. I am by myself. There is no one that I can call on for help and not many that I can confide in. Lord knows, I want to be supportive and helpful to those around me, and I will when I can, but right now I have to help myself.

Do Not Welcome Negativity

Do not welcome negativity. Do not put faith in your fears. You are powerful beyond measure and you need to control your thoughts. Favor is for a lifetime and your thoughts will rule your world. I was watching a recording of the Joel Osteen ministries on YouTube entitled "Don't Worry, Have Faith," and that broadcast inspired my spirit to write about negativity. It is amazing what you become accustomed to. It is even more amazing the number of people who claim the negativity in their life. Activate your faith, invite prosperity, increase and positivity into your life. Battle for your mindset and work on changing the way you think until it becomes impossible to sell yourself short. Why walk around discouraged or worried about something that hasn't happened, and nine times out of ten will never happen. I use to do that, and looking back over all that God has brought me through, I know that God's favor was on my side from the beginning. I just had to claim it.

Why I Write

It is not a game. When you pray, do not hold back. Be honest with yourself and God. He already knows what you are thinking, even the things your not saying. He knows all of your faults. Never hold back, even when you know you are wrong. Pray with respect to yourself and God, trust that your honesty will give you a breakthrough and release any limiting beliefs, frustrations, and dreams. Expand your way of thinking. Keep a journal. If you have a hard time finding the good in your life begin writing down what you are thankful for, and do it everyday. Trust me, once you write down your thoughts, prayers, and frustrations, it frees your mind for greatness. The weight of the world is no longer replaying in your head over and over again. I learned that I am thinking about a million things at once and I need to filter through all of my emotions. So now, not only do I write my books using my laptop, but I also have a binder where I physically write my prayers, goals and what I am thankful for each day. I also never say that I cannot do something. In my mind, I believe that I can achieve anything that I set my mind to; nothing is out of reach. I am not saying that it happens right away, but no matter what, I make a conscious effort to reach my goals. Writing is therapy for me. Typically, no one sees my struggle or knows what I am going through mentally, but when I write, I prove my vulnerability.

I advise that you write down everything, your thoughts, emotions, faults, gratitudes, prayers, etc. Get in the habit of letting go of your baggage and freeing up your mind so you can be focused on success. Whatever your version of success is, you have to train yourself to live the life of your dreams. Success is a habit and you become successful by discipline. *IT WILL NOT HAPPEN OVER NIGHT*, but it can happen this year if you remove negativity in your life and check yourself. You can be your own worst enemy and you need to decide right now that you are going to make an immediate change. Treat people with respect, stop being petty, be the change that your life needs to see. Now, if you get a check for being petty, undisciplined, and mediocre, then by all means continue your life and ignore this entire book. Otherwise, you need to get focused, create an outline for your life and dreams, then devise a plan to achieve it. Yes, you need an outline for your level of success, just like you need a business plan for any new venture you decide to take on. Your outline should not be set in stone. As you grow and become more aware of your actions, allow your mind to evolve and tap into what you buried, then change your plan for the better. You have no idea how much benefit can come from you treating people right, helping others, enjoying your life, and being able to bring your friends and family along for the ride. Consider your life your business and begin implementing a plan to achieve your goals. Once you achieve your goals but do not yet see a financial increase, please take a deep breath and relax. ***These things don't happen overnight.*** It could be time to change your perception, take a class or read a book about building your business, become a vendor at an expo or get a mentor. Just don't freak out. I am speaking from experience. God has a way of coming through for you in the clutch, but you have to work on trusting Him in advance when you can't see the victory ahead. I saw a quote one day while surfing through Instagram. It said, "You can't rush something that you want to last forever." My thoughts exactly. Be patient, pray hard, and imagine your life where you want it to be, then try again. Never settle, and remember that every setback is a setup to an even greater victory.

Commanding My Life

Pros and Cons

Does the good outweigh the bad? I was having a pretty good day, extremely exhausted and achy but all in all it was a great day. I didn't really beat myself up too much and anytime something negative came to mind, I redirected my thoughts to something positive and continued with my workday. I took a nap after work, did a short exercise routine and decided to head downstairs to make dinner. My roommate at the time left me a note saying, "I couldn't find your number, but I just wanted to remind you that the lease is up in two months." Immediately I felt the weight of the world was on my shoulders and I felt like I was going insane. I wanted to die and basically just quit life. I knew that this was another obstacle I had to overcome, so I took a deep breath and said to myself "Does the good outweigh the bad?" Lord, I hope so. I immediately began to pray, telling God that I could not see a way, but I thanked Him in advance for bringing me out better than I was before. I told him that this time I am not just going to get by, but I am going to triumph and have blessing after blessing and miracle after miracle and an abundance of favor. I claimed my victory in advance because God does not allow you to go through anything you cannot handle. Just because you don't see a way does not mean God cannot make it happen. Pray without ceasing, even when it is one more obstacle added to your week that you didn't need, or one more reminder of your obstacles that you didn't ask for. Cry, pray, and cry again. Let your emotions out, then work on your mindset. Listen to an inspirational message, talk to a counselor, talk to someone, pray some more, but please don't quit. Your life is not destined to be mediocre. The reason I will never give up, even when I don't have a dime, is because I know I am giving all I have every day. I will not just survive. I am going to live and enjoy my life and help as many people as I can along the way. I will never accept a life of mediocrity and I will keep following my dreams of becoming a successful realtor, writer, distributor and all around entrepreneur. You can make it too!

In Love

I have never been in love before and I know there is a part of me that wants to be. Call me crazy, but I feel like I need to be great as an individual before I can be great as a unit. I watch my siblings, family, and friends' relationships and there is really only one out of them all that inspires me to one day find love. Shout out to Gregory and Brittany Huggins. I don't believe in going against your spouse, or trying to one up your teammate, or cheating. If I want to have sex or be with someone else, I will, and if someone wants to do the same then I am too damn marketable to be with someone that doesn't want to be with me or vise versa. I understand having disputes, and arguing is healthy but not catastrophic. I believe communication can solve a lifetime of misunderstandings and more people should try it. I really want to be my spouse's wife, lover, girlfriend, teammate, best friend, business partner and more.

My idea of the man that I would want to build a relationship with is simple. He needs to be single, want a relationship, want to eventually get married, and put forth an effort in building a life together. I don't want a man that I have to raise. I want a man that knows how to pay bills, and makes me feel like no matter what, he has my best interest at heart, whether that is financially, emotionally, physically, or whatever. If I get drunk one night while out with my spouse having a good time; I won't have to worry about a thing. If my spouse has a goal that he wants to reach, I want him to tell me so we can make a plan together. I am not where I want to be financially, so I don't want to start a life with anyone, but God has a funny way of bringing people into your life when you least expect it, so I'm open to anything, but I am not settling for someone that doesn't stimulate me in all areas of my life. I am open to dating. There are not many people that I am intrigued by currently, but I am not so closed in that I won't introduce myself to someone I might want to date. That being said, finding someone to truly love is hard, but eventually God will show me who to pursue and it will be epic!

Your Surroundings

Hi and Bye approach. You will quickly learn which friends and family members are for you and against you. That is when you can express your dream, see the response and adjust who you give any more details to. There will be people in your life that you will no longer associate with period, ones that you will learn to keep at a distance, and ones that you will grow with and be close to. As your dreams evolve so does your circle of friends. Surround yourself with people doing better than yourself and never be the smartest person you know. If you are striving to be an entrepreneur, then those friends that have goals of working until they retire at 65, fulfilling their employer's dreams, will no longer be in your immediate circle of friends. That's just the way it is. Those people will no longer stimulate your mind because what you are striving for is completely different. Your whole focus will change and you will begin networking and reading about different successful entrepreneurs and learning how they achieved their dreams. That is when you need to begin your day with a wake up and win mentality. Create a morning routine that involves waking up before 8 a.m. and aligning your day for success.

I follow the life SAVERS from *The Miracle Morning* by Hal El Rod. I meditate to clear my mind, then pray to start my day with God. I say my affirmations once out loud and then once or twice in my head for memory. Next, I visualize my dreams coming to pass and write down what I am grateful for or I take time to write a new passage or poem for one of my books or personal journal entries. I typically read two books at a time. Currently I am reading *Think and Grow Rich* by Napoleon Hill and *Miracle Morning for Writers* by Hal El Rod and Steve Scott. Last but not least, I exercise. My routine is not in the normal order of the life SAVERS, but this set-up works better for my commitment to have a successful and prosperous day.

Regrets. I believe there is no such thing because everything you do is a choice. Who you choose to be around and take on your journey with you will directly affect how successful you become. If you have negative people around, killing every idea you have and not contributing to your life, then ultimately you will not succeed until you let them go. Just because you can't imagine working for someone your whole life and retiring with just enough to survive does not mean everyone is ready to live uncomfortable and chase their dreams. Do not give unwanted advice, especially to people who are comfortable being comfortable. Have you ever been to a seminar and there are people in the room that are true believers of creating their own destiny, then in the same room you have the skeptics who cannot think outside the box and who are not willing to imagine something bigger than themselves? Well on your journey to success, you will meet a lot of both types of people and it is your job to choose who you want to grow with or be mediocre with. Devise a plan for success, focus on your strengths, and enjoy the process. At one point, I was so busy just trying to make it while barely surviving that I lost my fun. I would feel bad when I did do something for me, thinking I could have saved that ten dollars and not seen a movie, or beat myself up mentally if I took an evening off and just sat up listening to my favorite songs. Do what stimulates your soul. If you wake up early then take an afternoon nap if you need it. Regroup and take some time for yourself and before you go to bed, plan your next day. Don't be the person that just lets life happen to them. Be the person who becomes the change they want to see in their life. Be so great at knocking down doors and making your goals happen that great people gravitate to you. Don't just endure your journey, enjoy it. In fact, take time out to visit a bookstore or Google books and people that have reached goals similar to yours, then do the same thing. You might find that it is easier or harder than you expected, but once you know, then you can decide on your next right move. That may involve taking a class, going back to school, getting a grant, changing your business plan, setting up a team, or starting over. Whatever you do, don't lose your joy. Enjoy the little things. Spend time with your family, find a mentor, life coach or teammate that you can express your feelings to while on your journey, and don't forget to start with self-improvement and changing the way you think.

Imagination

The one thing I love the most about myself is my imagination. I wrote over thirty fantasies in my first book, so clearly I can dream big and thinking outside the box is right up my alley. I'm about to boast on myself for a little bit. Every now and then, you have to look at yourself in the mirror and say, "Yep, I'm the shit!" with as much enthusiasm as possible. If I try to explain how my mind works, it will take a lifetime, so instead I am going to tell you why I believe that it is so easy for me to keep praying, dreaming of a better life is the only thing that keeps me from completely losing my mind. In a way, I think my imagination saves me. I use to think that my mind was going to eventually kill me because of how hard I thought my life was going. I use to beat myself up a lot in my head and would feel like I was destroying my body from the inside out. Looking back now, I have to brace my mind and realize the meaning of being fearfully and wonderfully made. You can think of the worst possible outcomes imaginable or you can change the world strategically. You can think of a billion dollar idea, and fall in love or you can harm yourself or others. It is so interesting how many thoughts and choices we make in a single day. You can choose to completely give up on life or look at the failure as another opportunity to learn a new way of doing things.

That idea right there is why successful entrepreneurs, lovers of life, and strong believers in God focus so hard on instilling in you the power of having the right mindset. Don't get me wrong, when you have had an endless number of setbacks, focusing on the positive and staying faithful is the furthest from your mind, but you never know when you are one prayer away from your break through and triumph. Wouldn't it be a shame to give up now?

The idea of having to rely on a man for money is one of my biggest fears. The second is settling for a life, a spouse, a job, or a lifestyle that I don't absolutely, without a doubt love. You get one life and it is so ridiculous to spend it with someone, or some job, or some life that doesn't make you extremely happy. Of course everyday isn't going to be sunshine and rainbows, but most of them can be. Living unhappy, miserable, sad, unforgiving, mediocre, and exhausted is for the birds. You are a human being with the power and ability to make a way out of no way. God is so much bigger than you and you are so much bigger than average, it is remarkable. Once you realize the way your God is set up, then you can realize that you have the power to be the change your life needs. Don't let another day go by without living to the fullest. Enjoy your life, seek God first, improve daily, and fight for the life of your dreams. Spiritual warfare is so real. The battle is ongoing and you are a champion.

Sex

I was trying to avoid this subject and I touched on it a little bit but I am being compelled to speak about sex before I can say this book is complete, so here it goes. Trust and believe I am not about to tell anyone not to have sex before marriage. Don't think this is about to be a passage telling you to wait, because it is not. However, if you are still a virgin, you should wait to have sex until you find someone that is going to respect you during the process. I was twenty years old when I lost my virginity and some of you probably think, "Damn, you were old!" Others might think it is good that I waited. Others still think I should have held out until marriage. Personally, now that I have had sex, I know that I want a partner that is compatible with me and that I can truly communicate with to meet my needs. If you can wait until marriage, pray hard and wait. I know it is not easy and if your imagination is anything like mine, it is incredibly hard to go without. I just want everyone to be smart and take care of their body. Don't be so quick to have sex with someone that is not adding value to your life spiritually, mentally, and financially. Soul ties are real and you have to watch who you are investing your time in. Remember people can only do what you allow, meaning, if you have someone that is mentally, physically, or emotionally causing you pain and you still continue to be around this person and having sex with them, then you are failing. Sex and love are two different things and you have to understand that sex does not mean the same thing to everybody. Find someone that can stimulate your soul and is a blessing to be around. Truly elevate your life and trust your body when it is telling you not to do something. Having sex is inevitable. It is going to happen eventually, so please know your body and if you are not ready then wait. Don't just have sex to be having sex. Just like the music I listen to, I feel like having sex with the right person should truly invoke an array of positive emotions. Your chemistry with the other person should be on fire, it should be fun and effortless. When you are with a person that can make you feel like you matter more than the BS and they can truly add value to your life, then have sex, but if not, then stop adding notches to your belt. You are going to have to learn this for yourself, just start making the right choices, work on your obedience to God, and make a conscious effort to change all aspects of your life for the better.

God Doesn't Call the Qualified; He Qualifies the Called

Sacrifice. I watch a lot of Joel Osteen broadcasts. He is truly inspirational to me and I thank God that I am able to receive His word through Joel. One day I was in the middle of the self-improvement portion of my day, reading *The Circle Maker* by Mark Batterson. In one of the passages, I came across the phrase "God doesn't call the qualified; He qualifies the called." That phrase has stuck with me and as they say, *it happens in threes*, and you should always follow God's promptings. Later that day I was scrolling through Facebook and my Durham, North Carolina Pastor Benji had posted a short video and I felt compelled to watch it. Literally the first thirty seconds of his message was "God doesn't call the qualified; He qualifies the called." Powerful! Once again, I said a prayer, just knowing that God was trying to tell me something. Later that evening my mind was still racing and I was feeling down that I was accomplishing a lot of goals but I was still broke. I decided to go on YouTube and turn on a Joel Osteen broadcast. Right after his classic joke, he went into his sermon and as I sat listening and praying I heard Joel start to say "God doesn't … ." I tell you, my eyes welled up with big ol' crocodile tears as I just sat there in disbelief. I could no longer see my computer screen through the tears and I just needed to pray and talk to God. I am my hardest critic. I always intend to be responsible and do the right thing and I always seem to fall short of a true victory. It is heartbreaking to have to settle every time something comes around. I've missed out on so many events and family functions and so on due to my financial situation that I am mentally dead, but God doesn't just speak to you when you pray. He gives you promptings all throughout the day and it is your job to listen and follow His instructions. I sat and cried, knowing God was telling me that this is only the beginning. I have a whole life of triumph ahead of me and I just have to stay in faith and work hard. I appreciate being inspired by the littlest of things and as I start to write, or research a new opportunity, or enhance my way of thinking, I know God is getting me prepared. I am ready, Lord.

It's Ok to Fail

It is okay to fail, but you have to get back up! Fail fast and fail forward. Most entrepreneurs who have already begun their journey will understand that message right away. I truly recommend a mentor, coach, accountability partner, etc. Find someone who will be a shoulder to lean on in this process. Keep going and don't discourage others whose dream isn't as big as yours, or perhaps is even nonexistent. I am speaking from experience. Other realtors would tell me that they wanted to make a $100,000 in GCI (Gross Commission Income) in real estate and I would think "Hell, you can make a $100,000 working in IT. You didn't have to get your real estate license to make $100,000." You can't make someone else work harder or dream bigger if it is not in them to do so. As much as women think they can change a man, it doesn't work with a man and it doesn't work with someone's dreams. Remember everyone's level of success is different and you have to reach your goal and encourage people, but don't inspire what is not there. You'll lose your mind, trust me. I am just telling you this so you don't have to go through it too. Just pray and continue to fight for your mind, body, soul, and spirit.

Anyone that has been praying for something to change or get better for years knows the scars that spiritual warfare leaves. Those who are not constantly seeking the Lord might confuse those battles and failures with just going through life. This is not true. It is a constant test of your faith. Will this break you or will this bring you closer to God? You cannot take anything on earth with you and you have such a short time to prepare for such a long time. Right now is when God is going to make or break you. Material items mean nothing and God is building His family. Your destination is everlasting life. Your mission is to not just barely make it. Your mission is to not to be mediocre. Start praying and building your relationship with God. It won't happen overnight and I have personally learned how to pray by seeking God, my daily devotional, other books, and different pastors along the way. I wanted to know God and His power. I am fearfully and wonderfully made and there is so much that makes me up as a woman. I think about sex, I get angry and mad and frustrated, I pray hard, I love my family and friends, I don't like people I don't know, I want to protect my family, I will soon be licensed to carry a firearm in the state of Florida, and anywhere else I can. I am imperfect and I am glad God didn't put the burden on me to be perfect. God, Jesus and the Holy Spirit know that you are not perfect too; but are you really working to build a relationship with God? I don't know if you heard, but there is a 100% chance that we are all going to die!!! Start right now, wherever you are and whole heartedly begin your relationship with finding God. Fail forward in all areas of your life. The one thing you cannot fail at is praying. If you can talk to other people, you can speak to God. I do recommend a daily devotional. My personal devotional is by the amazing Cindy Trimm entitled *Commanding your Morning*. Start there and expand. Meditate. Begin self-improvement and follow your passion. When you love to do it, it is not work. Trust me, you are going to make it! Just don't give up or stop praying before your victory.

Saved

April 1, 2012 was the day I was baptized at New Hope Church in Durham, North Carolina. Over 100 people were baptized with me in the pool or fountain in front of the church. I was nervous and happy and excited, all at the same time. I was ready and needed God to know, in front of everyone, that I was His humble servant. This book is providing me with the outlet to spread the word on how much I love God and how much God loves me. Can you imagine how great God is and how much He fights for His children everyday? Just thinking about God's love gives me strength and the courage to keep going. We must praise the Lord and seek the Lord forever. There is no right or wrong way to begin learning about God and how He speaks life over His children. I trust God and believe that He is going to bring me out better than I was before. I know He will continue to protect me and be there to listen when I have no one else. Love yourself, seek God, and build your faith. There is nobody greater or more powerful than God and I appreciate the victories of my life; past, present and future. I thank God in advance for showing up and showing out for me. I don't know when you are going to show up Lord, or how you're going to do it, but I walk by faith and not by sight and I truly thank you in advance.

Trust God

I know what you're thinking–trusting God no matter what is easier said than done. I wish you all knew me personally because you would know that I start over every day on my rollercoaster of trusting God. I feel like I'm in that movie *Ground Hog Day* and I am restarting the same day over and over with the same trust issues never learning my lesson. I know God has shown me favor so many times before and it is always in those moments of uncertainty that I forget how much God has really brought me through. I have been able to go to college out of state, my older brother Dwight drove me all the way to school. I had no other way there and I am so grateful that he packed up his car with all my stuff and lugged me down to school. I graduated college with a Bachelors of Arts in Business. I pay my bills, I have my real estate license, and I am a self-published author of two books, *Fantasy–Short Stories to Excite* and *Unwavered Faith*. I make moves, not excuses. I am ambitious and I have had so many challenges in life that I lost count, but I am still here. It would be an excuse to say that it is hard for me to trust God because of all the set-backs, lack, depression, etc. that goes on in my life. Trusting God **is a choice**. You either trust God or don't. This is where spiritual warfare plays the biggest part in my life. Trust and faith go hand and hand. You have to go to battle and get into the right frame of mind, that God will not allow you to go through something you couldn't handle. You have to believe that you can make it. You can't rush something that you want to last forever. This is one of the best sayings I've seen. It brings me back to reality and calms me down every time my faith is tested. Trusting God will by no means happen overnight, but you have to make a conscious effort to align your faith with God's word and practices. Be yourself. I already told you that we know you are not perfect. Just make the effort. It will become natural. You are human and we make mistakes, but God is going to show up and show out for you more than you can even fathom.

Success

Success–the accomplishment of an aim or purpose; the attainment of popularity or profit; a person or thing that achieves desired aims or attains prosperity. Achieving prosperity, abundance, and increase in every aspects of my life is when I will feel successful. No longer having to work for someone else, making their dreams come true. No more being mentally and physically restricted and limited. Earning an income doing everything that I've ever dreamed of. Expanding my real estate career, daily prospecting and receiving referrals from around the world. Growing my database and building relationships. Becoming a New York Times best-selling self-published author. Becoming a wife and partner to my future husband. Becoming a mother, having four or more children. Evolving my dreams while remaining success conscious with a constant desire to learn and grow spiritually, physically, intellectually, and financially. I have achieved so much in my life and I am grateful for taking risks and challenging myself. Learning to do whatever I am dreaming of, as scared as I might be. My goal is to never say, "What if?" I pray daily that my leaps of faith will bring prosperity in every aspect of my life. I love to write and take risks and embrace the thoughts that come into my mind. Accepting that I am not perfect and I can only do the best I can while striving for better gives me strength to keep going.

Adversity–difficulties, misfortune. I kid you not when I say adversity and I are like best friends. I feel sad when I see other people reaching their goals and earning a better income from their efforts. I look at myself and I can't help but think, is it my turn yet? I am grateful to be surviving, but I am constantly worried about the next hurdle. It seems like there is always something that is weighing heavy on my conscious. I pray for favor and mercy every night. I am grateful to survive and I'm glad for the people who don't mind working for someone else, I just don't want to do it. My prayers revolve around my finances and businesses. I investigate everything before I pursue it and I love doing research and learning about my next right move. Thank you God, for your strength that inspires me and gets me through each day. Praying for a change in my circumstances and staying in faith is not easy, but if it were easy everyone would be doing it. Do anything you can to grow your faith and follow the promise God has put in your heart. Remove "try" from your vocabulary. Don't intend to do better. Be better and learn more every day. Reaching your goals starts with daily self-improvement. Begin reading daily, working out regularly, meditating, and seeking God. Remember, *faith can move mountains.*

A Time to Live

Now for the sendoff. You are going to have ups and downs no matter what. Eventually you'll be in a position where it won't hurt so bad to go through a hurdle. It is a constant battle to improve yourself and live the life of your dreams. You have to suit up every day with the full armor of God. Praying through is about mentally, emotionally and physically programming yourself for greatness. Don't despise your small beginnings, nothing happens overnight. The key to living is to actually get up and start on your path to your dreams and goals. Don't just sit and wonder, get up and do something towards your goals everyday. **YOU HAVE TO LIVE UNCOMFORTABLE FOR A SEASON TO LIVE GREAT FOR A LIFETIME.** Never forget that. You are not going to be able to bring everyone with you; and everyone is not going to be as supportive on your journey to reach your goals, as you might hope. That's just a fact. Everyone's journey is going to be different. Don't settle or sell yourself short because of your circumstances. Your life was not meant to be mediocre, but you have to sacrifice, budget, and move more calculated than ever before. Promise me that you will consciously do something toward your goal every day. Once you reach you goal, don't be surprised when your next goal gets bigger and better. Expand your mind, read books to improve yourself mentally, emotionally, financially, spiritually, and relationally. Don't just endure life, make sure you enjoy it while on your journey to your goals. Take some time to yourself, as much as you can, and don't feel guilty about it. Remember the road to success is full of ups and down, twist and turns. Once you reach your goal, don't be surprised if your finances don't change immediately. Don't turn your back on your dream because the money wasn't immediate. Have patience, stay in faith and trust God. He is going to bring you out better than you were before. Remember, faith without work is dead; so get to work.

Writing is Therapy

"I can shake off everything as I write; my sorrows disappear; my courage is reborn." –Anne Frank

"Writing is a form of therapy; sometimes I wonder how all those who do not write, compose, or paint can manage to escape the madness, melancholic, the panic, and fear which is inherent in a human situation." –Graham Greene

"Writing songs is cheaper than going to therapy." –Brent Smith

"Start writing, no matter what. The water does not flow until the faucet is turned on." –Louis L 'Amour

"Sometimes you never know the value of a moment until it becomes a memory." –Dr. Seuss

"If I don't write to empty my mind, I go mad." –Lord Byron

"You have to live uncomfortable for a season to live great for a lifetime." –Tiffini Johnson

Contact the Author

f *FaceBook fan page:* @UnwaveredFaith

📷 *Instagram:* @_mrs__entrepreneur_

🐦 *Twitter:* @tiffini_j

www.ingramcontent.com/pod-product-compliance
Lightning Source LLC
Chambersburg PA
CBHW030823060726